DINOSAURS

Written by Kathie Billingslea Smith
Illustrated by James Seward

A Little Simon Book
Published by Simon & Schuster, Inc., New York

Created and manufactured by arrangement with Ottenheimer Publishers, Inc.
Copyright © 1987 by Ottenheimer Publishers, Inc.
All rights reserved including the right of reproduction in whole or in part in any form.
Published by LITTLE SIMON, a Division of Simon & Schuster, Inc.
Simon & Schuster Building, 1230 Avenue of the Americas, New York, New York 10020.
LITTLE SIMON and colophon are trademarks of Simon & Schuster, Inc.
Manufactured in Singapore.
10 9 8 7 6 5 4
ISBN: 0-671-63238-8

BRONTOSAURUS (Bron'toe sawr'us)

The name "Brontosaurus" means "thunder lizard," and the earth probably did shake with a noise like thunder when he passed by. This giant swamp dinosaur was seventy feet long and weighed 60,000 pounds, more than ten elephants!

Although Brontosaurus had a huge body, his head was quite small and housed a tiny brain. This small brain probably wasn't big enough to serve such a large animal. An extra nerve center in his tail helped control the movements of the back part of his body.

With his long neck, Brontosaurus was able to eat plants that grew on the ground or at the tops of trees. Scientists estimate that he ate 1,000 pounds of plants each day! Because his mouth was so small, he probably had to eat almost continually to stay alive.

Brontosaurus spent most of his time in or near water. The water helped to support his heavy body weight and provided a safe area in which to live. On land the slow-moving Brontosaurus was easily killed by hungry meat-eating dinosaurs like Allosaurus. Brontosaurus' only weapon was his long tail which could be used like a whip. Many Brontosaurus skeletons have been found with teeth from meat-eating dinosaurs stuck in their bones.

ALLOSAURUS (Al'lo sawr'us)

Long before Tyrannosaurus Rex appeared, Allosaurus was a much-feared meat-eating dinosaur. He stood fifteen feet tall, measured thirty-five feet long, and weighed about 8,000 pounds. With his strong claws and sharp teeth, Allosaurus could defeat giant plant eaters that were twice his size.

Allosaurus walked upright on his hind legs, balanced by his heavy tail. He could move quickly and easily overtake heavier, slower-moving animals. Both his large back legs and small front legs had sharp, hooked claws that he used to grab and hold his prey. His mouth was full of four-inch dagger-like teeth. When one tooth broke or fell out, another one grew in its place. With his wide jaws, Allosaurus could swallow huge chunks of flesh.

Scientists believe that Allosaurus hunted in packs. Groups of Allosaurus skeletons have been found in what are now Australia, Africa, North America, and Asia.

BRACHIOSAURUS (Brake'e o sawr'us)

Brachiosaurus was the largest of all the dinosaurs. He was forty feet tall, seventy-five feet long, and weighed about 170,000 pounds. That means Brachiosaurus was taller than a three-story building, longer than a tennis court, and weighed as much as 3,000 children put together!

Brachiosaurus was a plant eater and consumed over 2,000 pounds of food each day. His front legs were longer than his back ones, so he stood like a giraffe with his back sloping down toward his tail. He could stretch his long neck in all directions to reach ferns on the ground or leaves from the tallest trees.

Like Brontosaurus, Brachiosaurus spent most of his time in or near water. The water helped support his enormous weight and provided a safe haven from meat-eating dinosaurs. Brachiosaurus left the water only to search for food or to lay eggs. His nose was in a dome-shaped spot on top of his head. Some scientists think that he often waded into very deep water until only the top of his head poked above the surface — like the periscope on a submarine.

DIPLODOCUS (Di plod'o kus)

Diplodocus was the longest land animal ever to live on earth. Measuring ninety feet in length, he was as long as three school buses parked one in front of the other. But Diplodocus weighed only about 30,000 pounds and was much slimmer and lighter than Brontosaurus or Brachiosaurus. His great length was due mainly to his twenty-five foot long neck and his amazing forty-five foot long tail which was used like a whip.

Diplodocus was a plant eater and lived primarily in swampy areas. His brain was very small for such a large body. Like several other dinosaurs, Diplodocus had an extra nerve center on his spine to help control his tail and hind legs.

Scientists have found nests of Diplodocus eggs. The eggs were roundish in shape and measured about ten inches long.

STEGOSAURUS (Steg'o sawr'us)

The earliest plant-eating dinosaurs had little protection against the fierce meat eaters. But over millions of years, some plant eaters changed and developed shields and weapons of their own. Stegosaurus was one of these.

All along his curved spine there were double rows of tough triangular plates. These plates were one inch thick and two feet tall and helped to protect Stegosaurus. The plates also helped warm and cool the dinosaur's body as needed. Stegosaurus' main weapon was his ten-foot tail with four large spikes on the end of it. Each spike was three feet long and could easily rip open the stomach of a fierce meat-eating dinosaur.

Stegosaurus was twenty feet long and weighed 8,000 pounds. He would have fit in a space the size of a living room. He walked on all four legs and was low to the ground. Stegosaurus' brain was the size of a walnut. He relied on a larger nerve center in his spine to help control the movements of his back legs and tail.

ORNITHOMIMUS (Or'nith o my'mus)

The name "ornithomimus" means "like a bird." True to his name, Ornithomimus looked like a featherless ostrich and was about the same size as one. When he stood on his hind legs, he reached a height of about ten feet. His front legs were used for pulling and tearing food.

Ornithomimus had a beak like a bird's, but had no teeth. He couldn't chew food and probably swallowed insects, small animals and fruit whole. Many scientists think that Ornithomimus also ate the eggs of other dinosaurs. Fossils of Ornithomimus have been found in nests of petrified dinosaur eggs.

Ornithomimus could run faster than any other dinosaur. His speed was his only defense against hungry meat-eating dinosaurs. Ornithomimus lived in what are now North America and Asia.

TRACHODON (Track'o don)

Trachodon had a bill that looked like a duck's, so he is called a duckbill dinosaur. The broad duckbill had no teeth in the front, but jammed together along the sides were a total of 2,000 teeth! These were used to grind the twigs, leaves and seeds that were a part of his diet.

With a height of sixteen feet and a length of thirty feet, Trachodon was as tall as a house and as long as a city bus. He usually walked on his two larger hind legs and could run quickly, reaching speeds of thirty miles per hour. His two front feet were webbed.

Trachodon had keen senses of sight and smell. He stayed close to water for safety and could swim into deep water to escape hungry meat eaters. With his webbed feet, and long tail that was used like an oar, he was probably the best swimmer of all the dinosaurs.

Many trachodons must have roamed the earth. More of these skeletons have been found than of any other giant dinosaurs.

TYRANNOSAURUS REX
(Tie ran'o sawr'us Rex)

Tyrannosaurus Rex was the mightiest of the meat-eating dinosaurs. His name means "King of the Tyrant Lizards," and he was feared by all the other dinosaurs. His six-inch teeth had razor-sharp edges, and his strong jaws could crunch through bones and flesh as easily as scissors through paper. Tyrannosaurus was a fierce hunter and killed other dinosaurs, chomping the flesh off their bodies in hundred-pound chunks and gorging himself until he could eat no more. Then he would lie down and sleep for several days until, once again, he would awaken hungry and begin his search for food. Only the swiftest or best-protected dinosaurs, like Ankylosaurus or Triceratops, could sometimes escape from him with their lives.

Tyrannosaurus stood upright on his two back legs. His small front legs were useless. He was twenty-five feet tall and measured fifty feet from nose to tail. If people had lived in the time of the dinosaurs, a man would have reached only to Tyrannosaurus' knee. Tyrannosaurus was descended directly from Allosaurus, and the two dinosaurs looked very much alike.

TRICERATOPS (Tri cer'a tops)

Triceratops looked like an army tank, and when provoked, could turn into quite a fighting machine. He stood six feet tall, was thirty feet long and weighed about 16,000 pounds. His skull and neck were protected by a fan-shaped helmet of bone. Two three-foot long horns on his head and one shorter one on his nose stuck out like spears. The name "Triceratops" means "three horns-on-the-face." Triceratops was a plant eater and never used these horns to kill for food. But when attacked, he would lower his head and gore another dinosaur in self-defense. Triceratops was the only dinosaur that could sometimes defeat the terrible Tyrannosaurus Rex in battle.

Skeletons of Triceratops have been found in what are now Asia and North America. Although their hooked beaks were toothless, Triceratops had small, flat teeth at the back of their jaws. Scientists believe that they lived in marshes and ate tough plants and reeds that grew there.

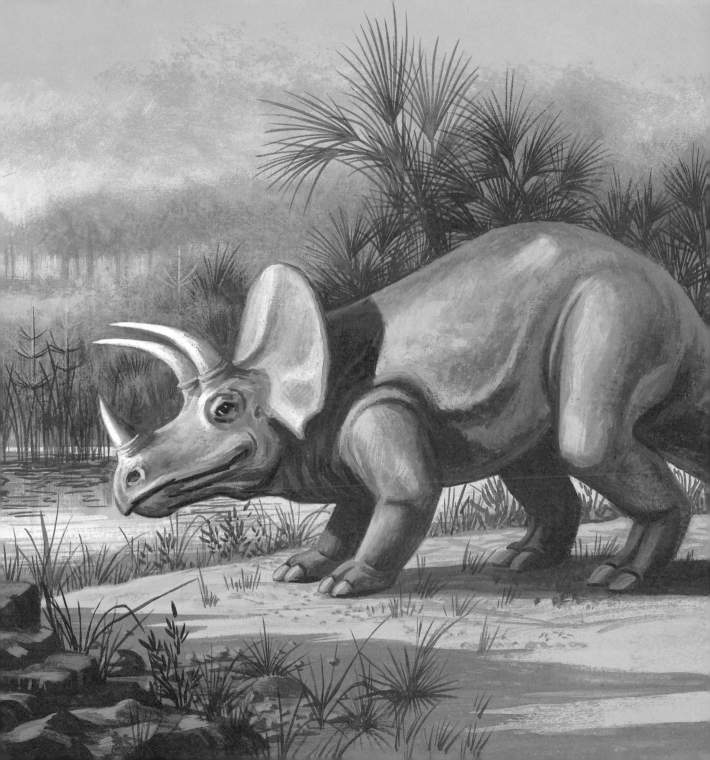

PTERANODON (Ter an'o don)

Pteranodon was one of the largest of the flying reptiles. Like birds of today, he had a small, light body and hollow bones. But Pteranodon had no feathers, just smooth skin stretched to form incredible wings spanning up to twenty-five feet. He probably sailed or glided through the air rather than flapping his wings to fly.

Pteranodon weighed twenty to forty pounds and most likely was white. He had a long triangular crest that pointed up from the back of his head and helped him to steer more carefully through the air. He must have looked like a flying dragon or a giant bat as he soared overhead. His excellent eyesight helped him to spot his prey from great distances. Pteranodon ate fruit, insects and fish. He had a neck pouch like pelicans do today and would fly over water and scoop up fish with his long, toothless beak. Many Pteranodon skeletons have been found in Kansas where, millions of years ago, there was a great inland sea.

ANKYLOSAURUS (An kyle'o sawr'us)

This giant plant eater looked a bit like a turtle. He was covered by an armored coat of heavy bone plates with sharp ridges. Pointed spikes stuck out from all sides of his body. Ankylosaurus also had a thick club-like tail that could pack a powerful punch against a hungry meat-eating dinosaur. When attacked, Ankylosaurus could simply crouch down on the ground. He was so well protected that most enemies learned to stay away from him.

Ankylosaurus measured about twenty feet long. He had small, flat teeth and ate soft plants that grew low to the ground. Scientists have found Ankylosaurus skeletons in many parts of the world.

STYRACOSAURUS (Sty rack'o sawr'us)

Styracosaurus is known as the "spike lizard." He was another of the horned dinosaurs. He measured about eighteen feet from head to tail. A bony shield, or frill, protected his neck. Pointing out from the frill were six long, sharp spikes. Another thick horn, or spike, tilted up from his nose. Styracosaurus was related to the Triceratops but was not as large, and not as good a fighter.

Like the other horned dinosaurs, Styracosaurus was a plant eater. He ate tough plants and reeds that grew in the marshes were he lived.